NEXT DOOR'S DOG IS A THERAPY DOG

DEDICATED TO DOGS.

WHERE WOULD WE BE WITHOUT THOSE
DOGGY SMILES AND WAGGING TAILS?

AND A HUGE THANK YOU TO
VIVIENNE DA SILVA FOR BRINGING
NEXT DOOR'S DOGS TO LIFE WITH
HER BEAUTIFUL ILLUSTRATIONS.

Gina

NEXT DOOR'S DOG IS A THERAPY DOG

GINA DAWSON

ILLUSTRATED BY
VIVIENNE DA SILVA

Leah loves the park. One day she asks Dad if she can go with Samson.

"I'll be safe with Samson," she says.

"No," Dad replies
"Samson is an obedient dog but
he's strong and doesn't like strangers,
so it's important that I come too."

5

Nan lives next door.
When Leah visits she enjoys
cooking, gardening and
playing with Monty.

Each week Nan and Monty
visit people in hospital.

Today Leah is going too.

She brushes Monty's fur until it shines.
"Monty really likes cuddles," says Leah.

"Monty is friendly and loves meeting people," replies Nan.
"He makes people feel better."

"Are all friendly dogs allowed in the hospital?" asks Leah.

"No," says Nan. "But Monty is a Therapy Dog. It's important that Therapy Dogs are gentle, obedient, behave safely and enjoy cuddling strangers. Not every dog does."

"Samson doesn't like strangers," grumbles Leah.

"Samson loves and protects your family," says Nan. "That's important too."

"I like that Samson looks after me. He's always pleased to see me," agrees Leah. "So how does Monty make people feel better?"

"You'll see," says Nan. "Let's go."

At the hospital people look at Monty and smile.

Nan knocks on a door.

"Hello, Mr Evans," she says.

Mr Evans seems sad. "Nice to have a visitor," he replies. Nan lifts Monty beside him.

"I had a dog when I was a boy," says Mr Evans. "We had fun together."

He strokes Monty, remembering his childhood .

"They were good times," he says, and he tells them of adventures he had as a boy with his dog.

"Come back soon," says Mr Evans when it's time for them to leave. "Monty makes me feel young again!"

"We will," says Nan, and Mr Evans settles into his pillow, smiling.

Leah looks at Nan.
"Mr Evans looked sad and now he's smiling," she says.

"People love to remember happy times," explains Nan, "and Monty helps them do just that. Now, let's see who's next."

Olivia feels tired and unwell.
Her parents can't visit today and
she needs rest. When she sees
Monty she reaches out her hand.

"When I'm better I'm allowed to have a dog,"
Olivia says. "I'll take him for walks and he'll sleep
in my room!"
And she asks Nan lots of questions
about how she looks after Monty.

"I'm going to hurry and get better!" Olivia says excitedly.
"I want a dog and he'll be the best
looked after dog in the world!"

After they leave, Olivia happily makes plans
before falling asleep and dreaming of the
dog she will have when she is well.

Leah looks at Nan.

"Monty gives hope," explains Nan.
"He's reminded Olivia that
she has lots to look forward to."

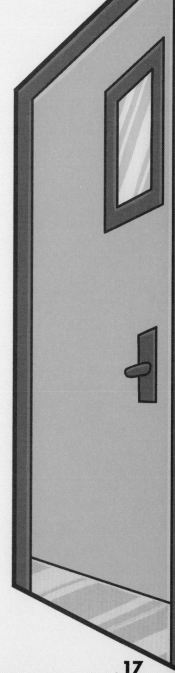

Maria feels upset. She looks
up when she sees Monty.

"Oh, what a dear little fellow," she
says. "I was just thinking about my
dog, Bella. I miss her so much! I
can't wait to go home to see her."

She holds out her arms and Monty snuggles in.

"It feels good to cuddle a dog again,"
Maria says, and she chats about Bella and
the games and cuddles they have together.

A nurse arrives and sees Maria laughing. "I've had such a lovely time with Monty!" she says. "I'm feeling quite chirpy again!"

Leah is amazed.

"Monty gives comfort," explains Nan. "Maria needed a cuddle, and now she feels better."

"Wow," says Leah, "Monty really does make people feel better!"

"Yes," says Nan. "That's why we visit. Some people here are sad or ill and Monty gives them something to smile about."

Their last stop is the hospital lounge.
People sit quietly while others chat.

"Here's Monty," someone calls out and the room becomes
noisy and cheerful as people pat, cuddle and talk to Monty.

When Monty reaches Captain Jennifer he raises his paw. "I'm going home tomorrow," Jennifer says. "Your visits have been lovely, Monty. Thank you."

Nan nods. "Thank you, Captain Jennifer," she says.

Back at Nan's house Leah says,
"Taking Monty visiting was fun!"

"Yes," agrees Nan. "Monty is good at his job
and it's lovely to see how he makes people
smile. Now, it's time to take you home."

Next door, Samson sees Leah and wags his tail.

"What have you learned today?" asks Dad.

"Well," says Leah. "I've learned that Monty is special because he gives hope and comfort and makes people smile. Samson is special too, because he loves and protects us."

Dad nods.

"Dogs are clever and very loyal," he says. "If we look after them and teach them their job, they'll happily do it every day. Some dogs are good at one job, some at another. It's a matter of having the right dog for the job!"

Leah gives Samson a hug. "Thanks for looking after me," she says. "I'll get your dinner!"

And everyone smiles.

NOTE TO PARENTS, CAREGIVERS AND EDUCATORS

The role of Therapy Dogs is to provide affection, comfort and improve well-being for people in a range of environments such as hospitals, aged care facilities, schools and kindergartens. They come in a variety of breeds and sizes, their common factor being an exceptional temperament.

Therapy dogs must be naturally friendly, confident, gentle, at ease in a range of settings and happy to be petted by unfamiliar people. They must remain calm around wheelchairs and devices, ignore food scraps or dropped medications and behave obediently for their own safety and that of the people they visit.

The positive effects of Therapy Dogs are broad-ranging as people talk, smile, remember, forget or relax. The dog's presence may lift moods, provide topics for discussion and motivate recovery.

Next Door's Dog is a Therapy Dog may be used to initiate a range of discussions with children – the first being the wonderful work that Therapy Dogs and their volunteer handlers do. You may choose to discuss the difference between Therapy Dogs and Service Dogs. Simply put, Service Dogs generally assist one person with a disability, work in public places and should never be distracted while working. Therapy Dogs help many people and enjoy petting, but may only go where invited.

Another discussion may be that of choosing a suitable breed of dog for a family, environment or job. Discuss how each breed has unique traits, temperaments, strengths and needs that must be met in order for the dog to live a happy and productive life.

There are opportunities to discuss the variety of roles that dogs with jobs play in modern society and finally, the topic of dog safety.

ABOUT THE AUTHOR

Author Gina Dawson has presented programs on a variety of social issues in schools for fifteen years. She is a lifelong lover of dogs, an experienced trainer and is cognizant of the disability sector. She is a volunteer for an Assistance Dog organisation.

Gina's passion is writing children's books that promote awareness about personal and social issues. *Next Door's Dog is a Therapy Dog* was written to educate children about the important role Therapy Dogs play within our society, bringing comfort and joy to people they meet.

In her spare time, Gina enjoys, in no particular order: dog training, reading, writing children's books and memoirs, walking, architecture, spending time with family and friends, and of course her dog.

Next Door's Dog is a Therapy Dog is her sixth book, and the third in the Next Door's Dog series.

ABOUT THE ILLUSTRATOR

Illustrator Vivienne da Silva has been drawing ever since she was old enough to hold a pencil. Inspired by countless animated films as a child, she scoured her local library for books on how to draw, and this ignited what became a lifelong passion. She still adores animated movies today, as well as dogs, tea, musicals and terrible puns.

Next Door's Dog is a Therapy Dog is her third illustrated book.

Other books by Gina Dawson

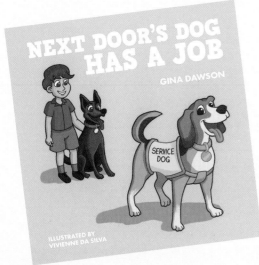

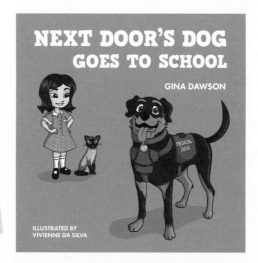

Next Door's Dog has a Job
ISBN: 9781921024870
Bailey is a very special dog.
He is a Service Dog. Join Tom as he
discovers exactly what that means,
and just how special Bailey is.

Next Door's Dog Goes to School
ISBN: 9781760790523
Grace wants to be able to do every-
thing other children do and now she
has Roxie she can. If Grace needs
help, Roxie knows exactly what to do.

So That's How I Began!
ISBN: 9781760790233
Modern-day families, body parts,
pregnancy and more – this is the book
to have on-hand for that moment a
child starts asking questions.

So That's What's Happening!
ISBN: 9781760791230
Suitable for boys and girls of any age,
this is a warm, all-inclusive introduction
to puberty that children will enjoy and
parents can relax about.

Supporting

Starlight
children's foundation

New Holland Publishers are proud supporters of the Starlight Children's Foundation

LOVABLE LOTTIE AND THE SHY SHEEP

ASIA UPWARD

ISBN: 9781760791308

A FLAIR for HAIR

Bilyana Di Costanzo
illustrations by Mauro Di Costanzo

ISBN: 9781760791223

CHARLIE'S SHELL

The tale of a little snail and the greatest shell there ever was.

Marina Zlatanova

ISBN: 9781760791377

A BESTSELLER FOR 55 YEARS
Now a Major Motion Picture

storm boy
the illustrated story

COLIN THIELE

ISBN: 9781760790622

A Boy and a Dog

A tale of finding true friendship

Illustrated by: Jenni Goodman

ISBN: 9781921024948

A FIRST BOOK OF AUSTRALIAN BACKYARD BIRD SONGS
Fred van Gessel

ISBN: 9781925546408

SMOKY
no ordinary war dog

Nigel Allsopp

Illustrations by Danielle Winicki

ISBN: 9781760791537

Baby Farm Animals

ISBN: 9781760791261

Narwhal's Friends of the Sea

ISBN: 9781760791254

Find these and other New Holland titles at your local bookstore. Sign up for the latest news and special offers or to buy online,
visit us at newhollandpublishers.com

NEW HOLLAND

First published in 2020 by New Holland Publishers
Sydney • Auckland

Level 1, 178 Fox Valley Road, Wahroonga 2076, Australia
5/39 Woodside Ave, Northcote, Auckland 0627, New Zealand

newhollandpublishers.com

A record of this book is held at the National Library of Australia.

ISBN 9781760791360

Group Managing Director: Fiona Schultz
Publisher: Francesca Roberts-Thomson
Designer: Yolanda la Gorcé
Project Editor: Liz Hardy
Production Director: Arlene Gippert
Printer: Toppan Leefung Printing Limited

10 9 8 7 6 5 4 3 2 1

Keep up with New Holland Publishers:
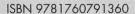 NewHollandPublishers
@newhollandpublishers

Supporting

New Holland Publishers are extremely proud supporters of the Starlight Children's Foundation and the purchase of this book generates proceeds to further help Starlight…
"Brighten the lives of seriously ill children and their families"
starlight.org.au

Starlight
children's foundation